Arthur's DREAM BOAT

Polly Dunbar

WALKER BOOKS
AND SUBSIDIARIES
LONDON • BOSTON • SYDNEY • AUCKLAND

One night Arthur
had a dream.

It was amazing.

"Wow!" said Arthur to his dog.

"Last night I had a dream."

"It was amazing,"
Arthur said to his brother.
"Last night I dreamt about
a pink and green boat
with a stripy mast."

TIPPETY

TAP

TIPPETY

TAP

"Mum," Arthur called.
"Last night I dreamt about
a boat. It was pink and green
with a stripy mast and
lovely spotty sails."

"Hey!" shouted Arthur to his sister. "Last night I dreamt about a boat. It was pink and green with a stripy mast and spotty sails, and it had a golden flag."

SPLITTER

SPLATTER

SPLODGE

"Dad!" cried Arthur.
"Last night I had a dream.
It was about a pink and green
boat with a stripy mast,
lovely spotty sails,
a golden flag and
a beautiful figurehead.

LISTEN TO ME!

I'm trying to tell you
about my ...

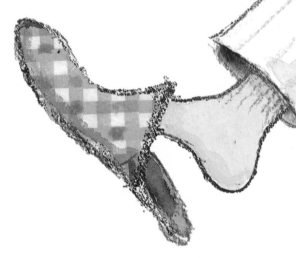

REAM
BOAT!

SSSHHH

SSSHHH SSSHHH

"Ahoy!"

"Arthur!"

ALL
ABOARD!

One night Arthur
had a dream.

And it really was ...

amazing!